Look up into the sky. Can you see the rainbow? It arches like a bridge over the hills and comes down into Nutshell Wood. At the end of the rainbow, deep in the wood, a tiny magical village is appearing. That village is Rainbow's End. Rainbow's End can only be seen by humans when a rainbow is in the sky, otherwise it is invisible to everyone except the gnomes who live there and the woodland animals.

The gnomes of Rainbow's End are jolly little folk who are always busy. Lots of exciting and interesting things happen in the village and no one is ever bored. This book tells the story of something that happened there. A little bird told me!

New Friends
Written by Jane Patience
Illustrated by John Patience

This 1987 edition published by Derrydale Books,
Distributed by Crown Publishers Inc.,
225 Park Avenue South, New York, N. Y. 10003.
© Peter Haddock Ltd: Rainbow's End Productions.
Printed in Hungary ISBN 0-517-64966-7

Pip and Woolly Foot were enjoying a game of leap frog in the warm May sunshine. Woolly Foot had just completed a particularly good leap over Pip's back when he heard his father calling to him. "Woolly Foot. Would you come round to the forge please, I need your help." Bristly was the blacksmith and Woolly Foot often helped him by working the bellows to heat up the fire. "Goodbye, Pip," he called. "I'll see you tomorrow."

Now Pip was feeling bored. All his friends were busy and he had no-one to play with. He wandered along the path. As he went he practised shooting his catapult, aiming up at the trees above. Then he heard a strange chattering sound. Looking up, he saw a red squirrel on a branch. It seemed very agitated and was making a lot of noise. "What's the matter with you?" Pip said in a cross voice. He aimed his catapult at the squirrel and shot a small stone at it. It scampered away and the next thing Pip knew, he was lying on the ground with all the breath knocked out of him.

"Well, that jolly well serves you right, you young rascal! I saw you shooting at that squirrel." It was Granny Rumbletummy returning home from the village. "You know," she said as she helped Pip up from the ground, "the squirrel was only trying to warn you to look where you were going, so that you wouldn't catch your foot down that hole." "Oh," said Pip sheepishly. "I thought it was just making a noise. Sorry." He called to the indignant squirrel who was back on a nearby branch. "I was in a bad mood because I haven't anyone to play with." The old woman looked surprised. "Well," she said. "Let's go and visit some of my friends."

Granny Rumbletummy led Pip off through the woods until they reached an area overgrown with bracken. "One of my best friends lives here," she said, tapping three times on the ground with her walking stick. A badger appeared and led Pip down a tunnel into its home which is called a set. Pip saw that the badger family home was very large, with many holes and tunnels leading off in different directions. Badgers are very clean animals and spend a lot of their time washing and the ferns and grass they sleep in are changed often, just as we change our bedclothes! Pip spent half-an-hour playing happily with the two badger cubs and then three taps on the earth above told him that Granny Rumbletummy was in a hurry to get on. "You can come back any time, to play with the little ones," said the badger as Pip made his way back up to the sunshine.

Next Granny Rumbletummy took Pip to the stream that ran through Nutshell Wood. "Can you guess who lives there?" she said, pointing to a hole in the bank. Pip peered inside and saw that the entrance was littered with old fish bones. "Ugh! A nasty, dirty animal," he said, wrinkling his nose in disgust. "I think you'll be surprised. Ah, here he comes now," replied the old woman. A flash of metallic blue-green darted past them and dived down into the water. A moment later the kingfisher sat on a branch with a fish in his beak. Pip was very impressed by the bird's swift flight and fishing skill. "No wonder you are called the King of Fishers," the boy said. "That's why I live so near to the stream – I must get plenty of practise. If you come to see me tomorrow I'll show you where all the best fishing spots are," said the bird. "Yes please," Pip replied.

Further along the stream, Pip and Granny Rumbletummy came to a part of the bank which was worn
smooth. "It's like a slide," said Pip. "That's exactly
what it is," Granny replied. "Do you know what
animal uses it?" Pip couldn't guess but he didn't have
to wait long to find out. He heard a high, squeaking
sound, rather like a bird, and then in a tumble of fur
three young otters, followed by their mother, slid
down the bank and splashed into the water. "I'll keep
an eye on the youngsters while you go to catch fish,"
said Granny. Pip enjoyed watching the young otters
playing in the water. He had never seen such good
swimmers. They could dive and swim underwater and
they loved their muddy slide. The mother otter re-
turned with a large trout and while her children ate
she gave Pip a ride on her back. "I'll give you swim-
ming lessons if you'd like," she said. "I certainly
would," Pip replied with a big smile.

Granny Rumbletummy then took Pip to her own cottage. "Now," she said, "I have something very interesting to show you, but first you must put on these special clothes." They both looked very funny in their strange hats and huge gloves. "These are my beehives," she explained. "Thousands of bees live in each one. I help them by providing a safe home and they provide me with lovely honey." She showed Pip inside a hive. He saw the large queen bee laying eggs which grow into more bees. There were lots of worker bees and Pip could see how they got their name. They do all the hard work for the hive, flying out to collect nectar from flowers to make honey and pollen to feed the young ones. The drone bees, who don't do any work at all, have a lazy life and are fed by the workers. "And now, young man," said the old woman, "I expect you are ready for something to eat and drink."

After a drink of cool apple juice and a honey sand-
wich, Pip set off for home, carrying a jar of honey
which Granny Rumbletummy had given him. Pip has
never been short of friends since that day and can
often be seen surrounded by woodland creatures.

RAINBOW'S END